ARE YOU YOU TINY?

Michelle Farnsworth

WestBow Press books may be ordered through booksellers or by contacting:

WestBow Press
A Division of Thomas Nelson & Zondervan
1663 Liberty Drive
Bloomington, IN 47403
www.westbowpress.com
844-714-3454

ISBN: 978-1-6642-6264-5 (sc)
ISBN: 978-1-6642-6266-9 (hc)
ISBN: 978-1-6642-6265-2 (e)

Library of Congress Control Number: 2022906288

Print information available on the last page.

WestBow Press rev. date: 04/20/2022

WESTBOW
PRESS®
A DIVISION OF THOMAS NELSON
& ZONDERVAN

To Harry and Tommy - my entire world.

To Richard - you know.

I am grateful for the upbringing I had with my grandparents, Florence and Arnold Engstrand.

Most of all, to my mother, Donna.
Who dedicated her all to me.

Are you tiny?

No. But I have a tiny leg.
I was made this way.
I love my tiny leg.

Are you tiny?

No. But I have
a tiny finger.
I was made
this way.
It's my magic
pinky!

Are you tiny?

No. But I have
a tiny arm.
I was made
this way.
I can do
anything
you can.

Are you tiny?

No. But I have
a tiny torso.
I was made this way.
I can scoot around
and play all day.

Are you tiny?

Are you tiny?

No. But I have tiny toes.

I was made this way.
I can balance all day.

Are you tiny?

No. But I have tiny knees.
I was made this way.
They touch each other, but my chair
helps me to sit and cruise around.

Are you tiny?

No. But I have
a tiny eye.
I was made
this way.
My glasses help
me to see all
the beauty in
the world.

Are you tiny?

Are you tiny?

No. But I have a
special brain.
I was born this way.
My brain always
sends messages
of love your way.

Are you tiny?

No. But I have a tiny dog.

He was made
that way.
He is my best friend
and guides my way!

Are you tiny?

YES!

But I'm mighty in so many ways.

CPSIA information can be obtained
at www.ICGtesting.com
Printed in the USA
LVHW071539290422
717566LV00009B/473